WILMETTE PUBLIC LIBRARY
1242 WILMETTE AVENUE
WILMETTE, IL 60091
847-256-5025

D1104212

The Opossum's Tale

WITHDRAWN
Wilmette Public Library

The Opossum's Tale

A GRANDMOTHER STORY

Story by Deborah L. Duvall

Drawings by Murv Jacob

University of New Mexico Press
Albuquerque

WILMETTE PUBLIC LIBRARY

To Baby Hannah

Artist's Note

This story, popularly told among Cherokees both in the southeast and in Indian Territory (now Oklahoma), was probably first written down in the late 1800s by ethnologist James Mooney. Several variants explain why the opossum's tail is hairless. In one, the hair clipping was done by Moth, and in another, the hair was removed by Snail using his magical powers. The Cricket version, however, is by far the most widely known. The original legend ends with the opossum lying on the dance ground as if dead, with a silly grin on his face. Our new version includes an original ending by Duvall wherein Si-qua the Opossum learns to make useful the tail he once saw as strictly ornamental.

— Murv Jacob

©2005 by the University of New Mexico Press
All rights reserved. Published 2005
11 10 09 08 07 06 05   1 2 3 4 5 6 7

Library of Congress Cataloging-in-Publication Data

Duvall, Deborah L., 1952–
   The opossum's tale / story by Deborah L. Duvall ; drawings by Murv Jacob.
      p. cm. — (Grandmother stories ; v. 7)
   ISBN 0-8263-3694-9 (cloth : alk. paper)
   1. Cherokee Indians—Folklore.   2. Opossums—Folklore.
I. Jacob, Murv, ill.   II. Title.   III. Series.

E99.C5D88 2005
398.24'529276'08997557—dc22

2005006285

Design by Melissa Tandysh
Printed in China by Everbest Printing Company Ltd. through Four Colour Imports, Ltd.

J398.2
NA
Cherokee

The Opossum, whose name in the Cherokee language is Si-qua, stepped ahead of the line of dancers. They circled round the fire as Si-qua sang loudly and in his best voice.

"See my tail, see it shine!"

"See his tail, see it shine!" repeated the dancers.

"See the fur, it is fine!" Si-qua chanted on.

"See the fur, it is fine!" the dancers sang.

Si-qua had waited all evening for his chance to lead the dance. The other animals groaned aloud when they saw Si-qua coming.

"Oh, no," the wolf named Wa-ya complained. "Now we have to sing another song about Si-qua's wonderful tail."

The song went on for four verses before Si-qua took his seat, as near to the fire as he could get. He took a comb from his pack and began to comb out his tail's thick, long fur. And the tail became even shinier, gleaming in the light of the fire.

Si-qua did not know that someone watched him from the trees. It was Ji-Stu the Rabbit. Ji-Stu always tried to make sure that he was the most popular dancer. He secretly admired Si-qua's tail, and this made him angry.

"Wake up, Ji-Stu!" Wa-ya the Wolf jumped beside him. "What are you dreaming about?"

"Oh, that Si-qua," Ji-Stu said. "Just look at him showing off."

"Maybe you should give him lessons, Ji-Stu. You are much better at showing off than he is. Just ask anyone!" Wa-ya laughed and waved goodbye.

Si-qua the Opossum talked with the dancers until they all left for their homes. He would sleep all day tomorrow, but tonight he stayed by the fire and practiced for hours singing a new song about his tail. From his hiding place in the trees, Ji-Stu heard the song, and he became even angrier. At last he slipped down the path toward home, grumbling with every step.

Ji-Stu awoke early a few days later. As Messenger for the forest, he carried all the news from house to house. Today he would announce that an animal council and dance would be held in four nights. As he walked down the river path his thoughts turned to Si-qua the Opossum and how he would flaunt his tail at the council dance. He thought so hard he tripped over the feet of Terrapin, the famous doctor, who sat dozing beneath a shady oak.

"Your head is out of step with your feet, Ji-Stu!" The big turtle pretended to look stern.

"Terrapin! How good it is to see you." Ji-Stu jumped to his feet and instantly thought of his excuse. "I was walking with my eyes closed to practice for the dance. If I can learn to dance with my eyes closed, I will not have to watch Si-qua carry on about his tail."

At that, the great Terrapin began to hoot loudly. "That is the best story you have come up with yet, Ji-Stu! Do not try to fool me. Instead take my advice. You need to go and visit Cricket!"

Ji-Stu told Terrapin about the council and dance and promised to stop by Cricket's house that evening. Cricket's neighbors sometimes called him the Barber because he knew everything about hairdressing. Maybe he could do something about Si-qua and his tail. Ji-Stu arrived at Cricket's house just as the sun was going down.

"Hello, Ji-Stu!" Cricket chirped. "What news do you have for me?"

"You are invited to the animal council and dance in four nights," Ji-Stu replied. "But I need your help right now, Cricket. Si-qua the Opossum is making me crazy. He brags endlessly about his tail. How can I stop him?"

Cricket rolled his eyes. How many times had he heard Ji-Stu brag about himself? But Ji-Stu was right. Si-qua's constant boasting bothered everyone. But what could Cricket do to really teach him a lesson? He settled down to think, and in a few moments he began to smile. Yes, he knew just what to do.

"Tell Si-qua that I will prepare his tail just before the council dance," he said.

Ji-Stu the Rabbit felt better knowing that Cricket would soon deal with Si-qua. He skipped lightly along the path to Si-qua's house as the sunlight faded. Si-qua would just now be getting out of bed. When Ji-Stu arrived, he found the opossum peering up into a persimmon tree.

"Good evening, Ji-Stu." Si-qua sighed. "How I wish I could get to those."

Si-qua pointed to four bunches of shiny black grapes hanging from a grapevine that had twined itself around a limb in the persimmon tree. "I try so hard to pick them, by holding to the limb, but they are just out of my reach. Maybe you could pick them for me."

"I have no time to work for you." Ji-Stu laughed. "But I do have a message for you. There is a council dance in four nights, and you are invited."

"Oh, thank you, Ji-Stu! Of course I will come. Everyone will want to hear my new songs about my tail."

"Yes." Ji-Stu grinned. "In fact, a secret friend of yours is sending the hairdresser Cricket over to comb your tail just before the dance!"

Four days later, just before dark, Ji-Stu stopped by to see Cricket to make sure he had not forgotten about Si-qua. Away down the path he could hear Cricket's music. How did he make such a loud chorus with only his wings? As Ji-Stu got closer he could hear Cricket's voice.

"I am the song of the evening," he sang, "I am the song of the night."

"Ji-Stu, I am just leaving to visit Si-qua," Cricket called to him. "Tonight you will be pleased with my work."

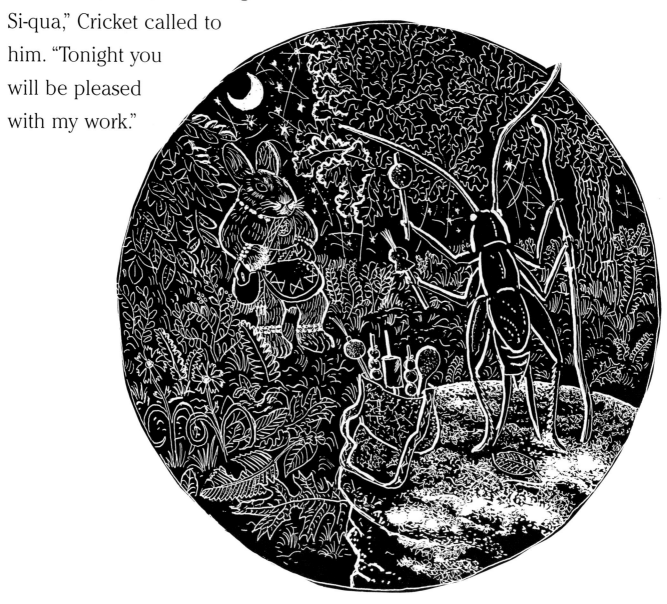

Cricket
hurried away to
find Si-qua already
awake and pacing nervously.
He had never allowed anyone else to touch his precious tail. Cricket
stood behind him and began to brush and comb the hair. Next he
wrapped the tail tightly with a buckskin strip from end to end. He
explained that the buckskin would keep the hair in place until the
dance began. But with every loop he made, Cricket skillfully cut
each hair down to the very root. And Si-qua never knew.

Si-qua walked slowly down the path to the dance grounds, being careful not to disturb the wrapping around his tail. What had Cricket said? He need only pull off the buckskin strip just before stepping into the circle of dancers. Then his tail would look its very best.

The dancing had already begun when Si-qua reached the fireside. There to greet him stood Ji-Stu the Rabbit and Terrapin.

"Do not go in just yet, Si-qua," Ji-Stu said, smiling. "We all want to get a good look at your tail. The next dance is for you alone."

All the dancers backed away from the fire when Ji-Stu announced Si-qua's dance. Si-qua held his head high as he pulled the wrapping loose from his tail, just the way Cricket had told him. Looking straight ahead, he walked proudly toward the fire and began to dance in a circle around it.

"Oh see what a beautiful tail is mine," Si-qua sang, and the dancers cheered wildly.

"How it glistens, how it shines," he continued, and the crowd grew louder still.

Si-qua could not believe his good fortune. At last his fellow dancers understood the wonder of his tail.

"Feast your eyes on every hair!" he cried.

"We want to, but they are not there!" yelled Ji-Stu the Rabbit, who had picked up Si-qua's buckskin strip and was waving it crazily in the air.

Si-qua looked around him. The other dancers were not cheering. They were laughing! With a growing sense of dread, Si-qua looked over his shoulder and down at what remained of his magnificent tail. He saw only bare skin. Si-qua could think of nothing to do or say, so he simply fell over on his back and lay there motionless, with a silly grin on his face.

Si-qua lay in that position until every other dancer went home. He could hear their laughter, still ringing in his ears. And what of his beautiful tail? The hair that fell off with the wrapping blew away on the breeze.

Si-qua trudged miserably down the path to his home. What would become of him now? He could not face his neighbors with such a horrible looking tail. Outside his house, he walked from tree to tree, unable to rest, unable to believe that his tail was lost.

"Look at my beautiful tail!" Si-qua cried out in despair. "It looks just like a snake!"

"Yes, it is most beautiful," came a voice from above. "It looks just like mine!"

Si-qua looked up to see Greensnake peering at him from a tree limb. "Oh Greensnake, what am I to do? I have lost my wonderful tail."

"Lost?" Greensnake replied. "Is that not your tail I see behind you?"

"No," Si-qua moaned. "My tail was beautiful and this tail is useless."

"Watch this, Si-qua!" Greensnake lowered her body, coil by coil, her tail wrapped securely around the tree limb.

"I can hang by my tail all day if I like. And so can you, now that you have a tail like mine."

Si-qua looked up at Greensnake, then back at his own tail. Then he ran to the persimmon tree. One shiny bunch of wild grapes still hung there, waiting for him.

"Greensnake," he said, "if I learn to hang by my tail, I can reach those grapes. Will you teach me?"

"Yes, Si-qua, I would like that. Meet me here tomorrow night and we will begin."

The next evening, Si-qua jumped eagerly out of his bed. Greensnake met him outside, just as promised, and pointed to a narrow limb growing just above the ground.

"The first thing you must learn," Greensnake said, "is how to coil your tail. We will start with this little limb."

Si-qua worked for hours, coiling and uncoiling his tail around the limb. He worked until he could control the tail without even thinking.

"Now you are ready to hang from a tree, Si-qua." Greensnake smiled.

"And I know just the tree!" Si-qua's voice squeaked with happiness.

Si-qua gathered dry leaves into a pile beneath the persimmon tree, in case he should fall. Up the tree he climbed, perching carefully on the limb that held the precious grapes. Then he coiled his tail around the limb and let go! What a wonderful feeling! Si-qua hung upside down, swinging in circles and laughing aloud.

"Wa-do! Thank you, Greensnake," Si-qua called down from the persimmon tree as he grabbed the bunch of shining grapes. "I will never complain about my tail again."

A few evenings later, Si-qua rose early to search for some choice walnuts down by the river. The sun was just going down when he heard a splash upstream, followed by loud screams for help.

From high in the walnut tree, Si-qua could see someone's head bobbing up and down in the swift water. The head had long ears attached. Ji-Stu the Rabbit! Si-qua had heard the stories of how Ji-Stu and Cricket worked together to destroy his tail. But now Ji-Stu was in real trouble.

Si-qua hurried down to a bend in the riverbank and found strong tree roots washed bare by the rushing water. The river would carry the rabbit by any second now. Si-qua coiled his tail tightly around the biggest root. As Ji-Stu's head came by him, Si-qua stretched out as far as he could and grabbed the long ears. Using all his strength, he dragged Ji-Stu out of the water and onto the riverbank.

"Si-qua, you rescued me, and I am so ashamed," Ji-Stu told him. "It was I who sent Cricket to shave off your tail. I hope you will forgive me."

To thank him, Ji-Stu arranged a special dance in Si-qua's honor. All his neighbors came to wish him well and to hear the story of how he saved Ji-Stu's life. When the moon was high, the first dance began. Leading the dancers was Ji-Stu, with Si-qua right behind him.

"See his tail, how smooth and strong," Ji-Stu the Rabbit sang. "See the tail of Si-qua!"

"It is sleek and it is long," he continued. "See the mighty Si-qua!"

On his way home, Si-qua came upon Terrapin, the great doctor, resting beneath his favorite oak tree. On one shoulder sat the hairdresser Cricket.

"Si-yo, Si-qua, hello." Terrapin rose to his feet. "Do you see how you have changed? Once you sang songs about yourself, but now your friends sing songs about you. Even Cricket!"

And Cricket raised his wings to make the music of the night.